Pink Pig goes to get some green grass.

His three friends do laps in the pond.

1

The three pigs tossed a hat.
Pink Pig said, "I need to fill
this bag."

The three pigs had been bad.
Pink Pig said, "That does not
help me!"

The pigs grinned and said "hi"
to their friend.
He did not see them.

Pink Pig handed them logs.
"Keep your logs," said the
three pigs.

Pink Pig has a soft bed.

What can the three pigs do to
get help?

Pink Pig lets them sleep in his
soft bed.

The End